Sassy Tomatoes

Claire Burbank

NEW HAMPSHIRE

1

I'm the only one. I'm the only one that isn't sassy. I always wonder why every tomato is sassy but me.

It was just a normal Saturday. I stayed in my shack until rush hour was over. I walked outside, all ready for work, when I saw the most sassiest tomato hopping towards me. I didn't want to get in his way! I hid behind the Porter Pottytow [paw-tea-toe] but Randall still found me. His face was more red than usual!

"Why did you stain Mrs. Stem's couch at the party last night, you couch tomato?" he asked me. "You broke the rules, you mischievous devil!"

"It was an accident," I replied, "now I have to get to work!"

"I don't care!" he answered. "Now you listen to me, you have to--"

"--get to work," I interrupted. "Now will you please move out of my path?"

"No, you're not the boss of me!" he whined. "You have to pay a fine of...uh, let's see...$10,000 first."

"Okay," I answered. I had a plan. "First, I have to go earn my paycheck at work."

See where I'm going with this?

"Fine," Randall snapped, rolling his eyes. "I'll be looking for you, Tina!"

"Okay," I agreed.

I hopped off to work so my sassy boss, Tim, wouldn't yell at me for being "late".

When work was done, I waited for rush hour to be over. When it was, I went outside. Guess who I saw? Randall, hopping towards me.

"He must want that paycheck I told him I had," I thought, hiding behind the Porter Pottytow again. Of course, he found me again because I hid there last time and he saw me hide behind it...both times.

"Tina...WHERE'S MY PAY-CHECK?!" he screamed.

I didn't answer. We stood there for a couple of seconds and I finally made a move. I sprinted. I hopped towards my house as fast as I could. He was trailing after me. I reached the door and went inside. I closed it as tight as I could. I was just about to lock it, but I had just remembered: none of my doors have locks. So I went upstairs and put pressure on my bedroom door when I was inside it so Randall couldn't break in. My chair and some baskets with stuffed animals in them were up against the entrance of my room.

I suddenly heard the sound of a door opening. I was sure Randall was in my room when I heard loud hops around the house. I <u>had</u> to made a plan to escape that sassy tomato. I just had to think.

2

I had finally come up with the perfect plan. I would jump outside the window!

Bang, bang, bang! I heard Randall trying to get the door open. Boy, was he loud! I opened the window and quietly jumped out. I landed with a THUD! Unfortunately, he heard me.

"What's going on in there?" he asked. Randall banged on the door some more. "What was that loud noise?"

Fortunately, he didn't know I wasn't in my room. In other words, he didn't know I was outside.

I hopped and hopped until I got to the gate that keeps bugs from getting in my yard. I opened it, and it made a loud creak. So loud that Randall heard it. He looked out the nearest window and saw me hopping on the street. He ran outside and started chasing me! I didn't notice he was until he was five feet away from me. I heard his elephant stomping. I went from walking to sprinting.

Suddenly we saw something unusual happening in the sky. I knew the weather-plants were right! There was a tornado, and it WASN'T a small one.

Randall ran away and he stayed safe and sound. My situation was the opposite. I got swept up with the tornado. I closed my eyes and prayed. A broccoli tree was about to hit me and I didn't even notice!

I am the luckiest tomato in the world to not die in that tornado. When it stopped, I safely landed on the ground. I did have a couple of bumps and bruised etc., but I was fine. I was so relieved that I didn't...well, you know.

"Wait a second," I thought.

Everything was fine--except for one little thing: I wasn't home anymore.

3

I knew I had gotten carried away the second I arrived at the strange place because it looked nothing like home. In fact, it looked like the <u>opposite</u> interior. While I was looking for help, suddenly I saw something small and red.

"Phew!" I thought, relieved. "Another tomato."

I started hopping towards it and my eyes

made out a small bow on the top of it's head.

"Okay then, it's a girl," I thought.

I saw it had a binky in it's mouth.

"Aw, it's a child, she can't help," I thought. "I better keep looking."

"What are you doing here?" she snapped. "You're intruding my town!"

"No, no, it's not what it looks like--" I answered.

"-- Oh, I think it is," she interrupted.

This was an extra sassy tomato!

"No, there was a tornado, and I, um...," I explained, trembling, "got carried away from home."

I would have never thought I would be afraid of a small tomato like I was!

"Uh, liar, liar, pants on fire!" she replied. "You just came here because you want to live in this beautiful town. Well, your terrible plan didn't work, missy! Nobody lives in this town but me and daddy."

"No, I'm not lying--wait, so you're saying nobody lives in this <u>huge</u> town but...you and your dad?" I asked, confused.

"First of all you ARE lying, I've seen and heard all of the liars say that," she pouted like she was smarter than me, "and second of all: what's the surprise?"

"It's just that...normal tomatoes don't have a town all to themselves," I retorted as nice as I could.

"Don't get all sassy with me, missy!" she shouted. "Now get out of <u>MY</u> TOWN!"

"I can't," I told her. "I can't without a guide to <u>MY</u> home."

We stood there for a couple of seconds, me smiling and her thinking.

"FINE!" she screamed.

I jumped back.

"Let's just go to my daddy to get a map," she muttered, madly.

"At least she's calmed down," I thought.

So we headed off to her... "daddy". Hope-fully the apple doesn't fall far from the tree!

4

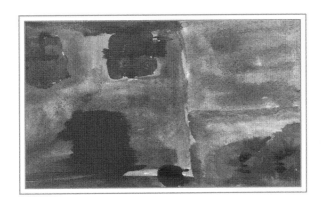

When we arrived at a gigantic mansion, we entered it. Everything in that place looked like it was owned by a really rich tomato. We walked down an indescribable hall that lead to a ginormous bedroom. It had special pottery on shelves and and ancient-looking necklaces hanging on mannequins all over the room. The bed was about the size of my shack. It was standing in the middle of the room. It was very tall and fancy. There were curtains hanging from the ceiling to the floor, covering the bed completely. I was shocked when I came in. It took a little bit for me to examine it and take it all in, when I was startled by a loud shout.

"DADDY!" the small, sassy tomato I met earlier screamed. You know, the one that called ME sassy. Sure, I'M the sassy one...ANYWAY!

"What, my darling?" a voice answered quietly. He said it like a statement, but I knew it was a question by heart. You know, being the best at grammar in elementary school, not to complement myself or anything.

Back to the story!

"We need a map!" the child tomato demanded. She stomped her foot while shouting.

We still couldn't see her "daddy" because he was behind the curtains. I didn't know if it was up high or down low.

A small map slid from under the curtain.

"Bigger!" she screamed.

While the big guy behind the shades searched for or made a map (I don't know what he was doing), I asked a question that was bugging me for a while to the little tomato: "What's your name?"

"Diva," she answered.

"No surprise there," I muttered.

"Hmm?" Diva asked. "Did you SAY something?"

"Uh, no," I replied. "Nothing at all."

I bit my lip. There was silence for a few seconds.

"Okay," she finally agreed.

I sighed with relief. She would probably have a fit if she found out what I had said about her. Just like a diva.

A gigantic map slid from underneath the curtain.

"Thanks, daddy!" Diva shouted. "Bye, bye?"

She started to head outside the bed-room but I stayed behind, watching her drag that huge map. She had to come back into the room to grab my arm be-cause I was looking at the antique pots.

After she dragged me out of that place, I looked at the map several times and I didn't see "Sassafrass" on there (the name of my town)!

"SO," Diva asked me, "which one is your town?"

"It's not on there," I answered, staring blankly at the contruction paper.

She groaned. "Are there any towns on here close to yours?"

"Yeah, but it's not in Sas Diego," I explained.

"Well, which one is it?" she demanded.

"Sassingham," I replied. "It should be right across The Tomexas Bridge near Plantsberg."

"Okay," said Diva, looking and pointing at the map, "that's only...102 miles away!"

How sassy can a tomato get?

"Okay, perfect," I said, "let's go!"

Diva rolled her eyes and muttered, "Can't these peasant-tomatoes get sarcasm?"

She thought I couldn't hear her...but I DID.

I turned around and gave her a cold stare. "Did you just call me...a peasant-tomato?"

"Uh, maybe," she answered, sounding a bit...scared!

I guess my stare really gave off a scare!

So we headed off to the Tomexas bridge.

Two minutes on our way, Diva started complaining.

"Ugh, how much longer?" she groaned.

"I don't know," I replied.

"How much longer?!" she demanded. "I don't know," I repeated as calm as I could.

"HOW MUCH LONGER?!"

"I don't know."

"How much longer?"

"I don't know."

"HOW...MUCH...LONGER?!!?!?!"

I was prepared. I took my earplugs out of my bag and put them on. I could still hear her mu"ed voice through the blocking.

Five minutes later, we saw a building. By then, Diva was on my shoulders, me carrying her.

"This looks like Sas Diego Grill!" she exclaimed, pointing at the map. "Let's go in, I'm starving!"

"Okay," I agreed. I figured she would pay, you know, having her own town and all.

We went inside and saw very few vegetables there.

"Ew, restaurants with no tomatoes are gross," Diva said.

"Hey, don't judge a book by its cover," I told her, setting her down on the ground.

"Don't tell me what to do," she pouted.

"Diva, now is NOT the time," I scolded.

"Fine," she answered.

A hostess seated us and we ordered our drinks.

A tomato sitting next to us was eating

loudly and we couldn't help looking at him. He had yellow skin and a silly hat on.

"What are you looking at?" he said looking behind him to see what was going on.

"Oh, nothing, sir," I answered for us.

Diva rolled her eyes. We waited awkwardly for our drinks while the guy munched on his meal very loudly. After about ten seconds he shouted, "I'm Lemur!"

We just carried on with our lives, not knowing he was talking to us. It was still silent.

"I'm Lemur!" he repeated.

Ten seconds later, he introduced

himself again. We were silent until "Lemur" got impatient.

"Come on, I'm talking to you!" he finally shouted with his strong, western accent.

I looked at him and asked, "Us?"

"Yes, you!" he replied. "What're you doin' in a fancy restaurant like this?"

We looked around and Diva and I saw a very un-fancy place.

"I could ask you the same thing...except I couldn't because this is NOT a fancy place," Diva answered while our waiter placed our drinks on the table.

Diva was staring coldly at Lemur but I elbowed her to make her stop.

"We just needed a place to eat," I exclaimed. I took a sip of my Shirley Tempato. "We have a big adventure ahead of us."

"Really," he replied. "Where're ya' headin'?" Lemur took a sip of his Lemonato.

"The Tomexas Bridge," I answered.

"What?" he gasped. "Only a tomato with an itty-bitty-brain would even think to cross the TOMEXAS bridge!"

"Excuse ME, are you...calling me...STUPID?!" Diva screamed. She looked at the waitress who backed up into the kitchen, afraid to take our orders.

"Woah, woah, I want no trouble here," Lemur told us. "I'm just saying, you have to have the right tools and...skills."

"Are you saying that we <u>don't</u> have the right tools and skills?" I asked him, starting to get angry.

"No, ma'am, I'm just saying you might need someone...like me," he said, smiling.

Diva clenched her fist.

"If you think you have the stuff why don't you come with us?" I replied, smirking.

"What?" Diva shouted. She was confused.

I winked at her and whispered, "I've got a plan."

5

After we finished our food, we headed off and out to The Tomexas Bridge.

"Ugh, WHHYYY do we have to go so far?" Diva asked impatiently.

"You wanted me out of your town," I reminded her.

"Oh," she answered, "well...why do you have to live so far away?"

It was almost like she was thinking of

ways to be sassy to me.

"Well so_RRY_ that I live somewhere be-sides near you," I replied, starting to get a little sassy.

"Oh, no," I thought. "Sassy tomatoes made non-sassy tomatoes sassy! And me and Lemur are the last un-sassy tomatoes on earth!!!"

I was going so crazy, I was using bad grammar!

"I hate to interrupt your argument, but we have a little problem," Lemur told us.

He pointed in front us. Diva and I turned around and saw a broken bridge. The water looked VERY deep.

"What're we gonna do?" I asked them.

"Leave?" Diva suggested. "Give up? If you wanna turn around raise your hand."

We stared at her coldly as she raised her hand.

"Now child, we didn't make it this far to give up, did we?" Lemur answered.

"Maybe?" Diva replied, smiling all angel-like.

"No, we're not giving up," I argued, just in case Lemur gave in to her negativity. "This bridge has to be a <u>little</u> bit sturdy, I mean, it's The Tomexas Bridge, the state's capital bridge, the best physical feature in the WHOLE ENTIRE UNIVERSE!!!"

See? Coo coo!

"Okay, then cross it," Diva scoffed, rolling her eyes.

I took a deep breath and said, "Okay." I hopped on the bridge as light as I could. The bridge was completely out of order, I could never cross it without ...jumping.

I gulped at that thought, butterflies swarming in my stomach.

"Guys," I said out loud. "I think I have to...run and jump."

"Are you crazy?!" Lemur shouted. His voice was so loud, it echoed! It collapsed the rest of the bridge clean off! There was no bridge to run and jump off!

"What're we gonna do?" I panicked. "I have to get home, guys!"

"Thanks to Lemur, you can't leave my beautiful town and get back to your family," Diva agreed. "Ugh, Daddy's gonna be so mad!"

"I don't have a family, I just need to...get back to my home," I told her. I thought for a second. "Now that I think about it, I don't have any friends to get back to either."

"So, maybe it wouldn't be so bad to live somewhere else, huh?" Lemur added. Him and I looked over to Diva.

"What?" she asked.

"You know what," I answered. Diva thought for a second, looking at the sky. She tapped her chin.

When she finally figured it out, Diva said, "No."

"Yes," Lemur disagreed.

"No!" she repeated, whining.

"There's no other choice," I told her.

"Uh, how about we look for another town?" she suggested.

I looked at the sky. It was getting pretty dark.

"I can tell the sun is going to set very soon," I noticed. I turned to Lemur. "Do you know anywhere we could stay?"

"I do, but we couldn't reach the place before the sun sets," he explained. "We might as well just sleep on the ground."

Diva laughed.

"You're laughing pretty hard considering that wasn't a joke," I said to her.

She stopped laughing. "What?"

"I'm serious," Lemur replied.

Diva fainted.

"We might as well leave her like that for the night," Lemur suggested.

I nodded, agreeing.

We gathered piles of leaves and made a big bed. We fell asleep peacefully.

6

That morning, I woke up to the sizzling of bacon on the grill. Diva was right where I left her. I stood up, yawned, and went over to her. Her chest was rising. Uh, not that I cared, or anything. She was a pain, anyway.

"Would you like some pigs butt?" Lemur asked, trying to speak over the sizzling.

"That's not something you hear every-day," I replied. "Where'd you get that ba-con?"

"I got some from the restaurant," he answered. "Always have to stalk up on food for an adventure. I have some hamburgers for lunch."

Diva woke up at the word "hamburger" and gagged.

"Don't even speak of that disgusting grub you call 'food'," she said, wide awake.

"Well, after breakfast we can get going and at lunchtime you could just have poison berries," I told her.

"You know, maybe the bun wouldn't be

so bad," she said quickly.

"Great, then let's go!" Lemur exclaimed.

We headed off with no problems, until we heard a sound. A very interesting sound. We didn't find out that it was a yo-del until we got closer to it. We followed a path until we saw a small, cozy town. The tomato kept yodeling and yodeling until it started to bug Diva.

"SHUT UP!" she shouted unkindly.

"Diva, mind your manners!" I com-manded. "That was rude!"

"Sorry, I couldn't take it anymore!" Diva pouted, crossing her arms.

"Aw, it's alright," the yodeler replied.

"What are you doing in a fine town like this?"

"Well, we were trying to find my home because I'm lost," I explained, "but then I realized I really have nothing to lose and now I just want a new home."

"What about your family?" the yodeler asked.

"I don't have one, for the last time!" I shouted.

Everything was silent. I went from mad to sad. "I just don't know what to do."

I saw Diva with the tiniest bit of pity in her eyes. She snapped out of it and said, "Okay, so can she stay here?"

"I don't know, you're going to have to

ask the mayor," he replied.

I was just about to ask Diva if she could bribe with money, but I had just remembered, we left it at the bridge.

I sighed.

"Well, just another adventure waiting to happen!" Lemur exclaimed.

"More like a broken arm waiting to happen," I heard Diva mutter.

I rolled my eyes and we headed off to the mayor. I hoped and hoped that the mayor wasn't sassy...but just hoping didn't work out so well.

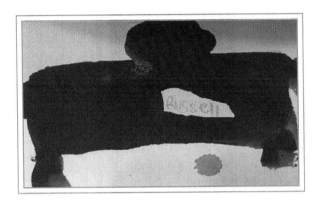

7

We headed off to town hall with pep in our step. I was excited for a new home, Diva was excited to never see me again, and Lemur wanted adventure. When we opened the door of the building, we saw the mayor at his desk. He had a silver plaque on it that said, "Mayor Russell".

"Um, excuse me?" I said to him. "Sir?" The mayor looked up. "How may I help you?"

"Well, I'm sorta-kinda homeless, and I was sorta-kinda wondering if you could sorta-kinda spare a home for me in this town?" I replied, sheepishly.

I gulped.

"Absolutely!" he exclaimed.

We all smiled.

"Not," he added, his peppy look fading away.

"What?" Lemur asked. "Why?"

"I'm not letting a hobo crash into my town randomly," Russell answered.

"Well, this 'hobo' got carried away in a tornado and landed up in my town," Diva interrupted, "so just let the poor thing stay in a cottage or ELSE..."

I guess the mayor didn't want to know <u>what</u> else, because he agreed to let me stay...shivering.

He led us to a nice, small cottage and showed us around. Until it was time for Lemur and Diva to...go.

"Well, I guess it's time for us to head out," Lemur said.

My face went from happy and excited to sad and melancholy. I was sad about my friends leaving...even Diva! I would miss her sassy outbursts and her controlling finger always pointing in the direction behind her. And Lemur. I would miss his funny accent and his love for adventure.

"Home," I thought to myself, "or friends?"

I hugged Lemur awkwardly and high-fived Diva. I had guessed it was goodbye. We all sighed (except for the mayor, of course). It was probably the second most sad thing in my life...don't ask.

"Bye," I said to them softly as they headed off into different directions.

By the time the mayor was done, the sun was almost completely down.

"Thank you," I said to him. I yawned.

"Have a good night," Russell said sarcastically. At least he was <u>trying</u> to be nice.

I went inside my new cottage and lay in my bed. I let out a big sigh and started to snooze off. I had a feeling the next day would be a loooong first day at my new town.

8

I woke up, my alarm booming. I raced to get ready for my first day at my new town. I was so excited, I wore my lettuce hat! I left my new home and went to my new job that I got when the mayor and I were touring the baby doll factory. I bursted out the door, carrying my work bag as the cold breeze bit at my face. I was probably the only one running in the whole town. Everyone was grumpy, walking slowly with slump in their shoulders. I started getting slower because I wanted to fit in with my new community. I wanted to make a good impression.

Suddenly, I remembered. Lemur and I are the only non-sassy tomatoes ever!

"Well, maybe I'll find <u>someone</u> like us," I thought. "There has to be at least <u>one</u> tomato that's nice in this town."

I started to feel more confident when I saw the tomatoes in that town. There was so many, there had to be at least <u>five</u> like me! I smiled and then remembered, fit in.

I was wearing a grumpy face until I got to the factory.

"Hello, fellow tomatoes!" I announced, walking into the huge building.

"Ssh!" some elderly tomato hushed.

"Yeah, we're trying to work here!" another exclaimed, harshly.

"Okay," I replied softly, "sorry."

Gloomily, I started making baby tomato dolls. Accidentally, I made my first one have a frown instead of a smile.

After my terrible day at work, I went home and lay in my bed.

"Holy guacamole," I sighed.

"Excuse me, town of Sassingham!" I heard the mayor announce on a speaker. "Any newbies come to town hall immediately for a, uh...discussion."

He said it firmly, which meant I had to go the second he finished talking. I rushed down to town hall as fast as I could. I burst through the door and realized...I was the only one there.

"I knew you were the only newbie in town," the mayor started, "but I didn't want you to suspect anything suspicious."

"What's going on?" I asked, backing up from his desk.

Russell stood up from his chair and suddenly ripped off his mayor costume.

"Randall?"

9

I couldn't believe my eyes. Was I seeing things? Was I dreaming?

"Where did you come from?" I beamed. "What's happening right now?"

"Let's just say you weren't the only tomato in that tornado," he answered. "I did a little sneaking around if you know what I mean."

"Well, what d'ya want from me?" I replied, worriedly.

"I think you know," he explained.

"No, I don't," I disagreed.

"Okay, I'll give you a hint then," he replied. "Stain...couch...paycheck."

I rolled my eyes. "Oh my gosh, that again?"

"My brother had to get a new couch," he replied. "They only came in...beige!"

"Well, are you gonna let me out?" I asked.

"Pft!" Randall sco!ed. "I think you can answer that question yourself."

There was an awkward silence.

"So...that's a, uh...no?" I said.

"Of course it's a no!" he yelled suddenly.

I jumped.

Soon I was tied in roped in a chair.

"Can't I just give you the paycheck now?" I asked.

"Nope," Randall answered. "The beige is bought."

I struggled to escape from the ropes. Nothing worked.

"Well, that's fortunate," I muttered as Diva and Lemur bursted through the doors of the building.

I watched Lemur untie me and Diva kick Randall's butt. Soon he was on the floor and the heroes and I exited the town with glee. We all went to Diva's town to go to the food court.

"Thank you guys so much for saving me!" I exclaimed, hugging them. "But, why did you come?"

"We wanted to see how your first day was going but we didn't see you in your cottage," Lemur answered. "So we were gonna ask the mayor where you were when you were tied up in ropes, so we saved you."

"Oh, that was so nice!" I exclaimed. "Except...we still have one teeny problem."

"I think I know what it is," said Diva, beckoning me. "Come on, I need to show you something."

I threw my frozen yogurt cup in the trash and followed her. Lemur trailed after us after throwing his chicken finger basket in the trash.

Diva lead us to a huge house right next to her mansion.

"What is this?" I asked, even though I totally knew what it was!

"Your new house!" Lemur exclaimed.

"Oh, my gosh!" I replied. "It's wonderful, thank you!"

I hugged both of them tightly. "You guys are the best of friends I could ever ask for."

"I'm your...friend?" Diva wondered out loud.

I glanced at my house then back at her. "How couldn't you be?"

Acknowledgements:
Shea Hanifin for inventing
Sassy Tomatoes;

Bill Burbank for encouraging me
and making the publishing happen;

The rest of my family for
supporting me;

Faelynne Johnson for the wonderful
picture (on the next page)

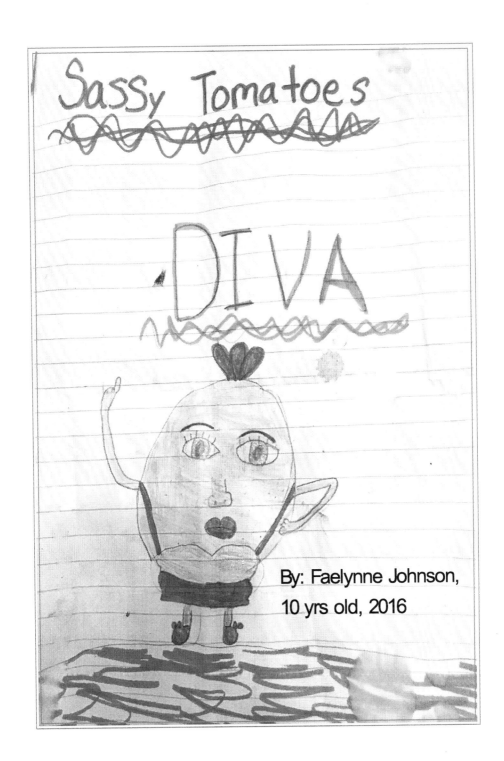

By: Faelynne Johnson, 10 yrs old, 2016

Made in the USA
Middletown, DE
08 May 2018